HO'ONANI
HULA WARRIOR

Heather Gale   *illustrated by* Mika Song

tundra

To my mom, who taught us to love people
for who they are — HG

To Small Grandma, who always cooked dinner — MS

Text copyright © 2019 by Heather Gale
Illustrations copyright © 2019 by Mika Song

Tundra Books, an imprint of Penguin Random House Canada Young Readers,
a Penguin Random House Company

Library and Archives Canada Cataloguing in Publication

Gale, Heather (Children's author), author
    Hoʻonani : hula warrior / Heather Gale ; illustrated by Mika Song.

Issued in print and electronic formats.
ISBN 978-0-7352-6449-6 (hardcover).—ISBN 978-0-7352-6450-2 (EPUB)

    1. Kamai, Hoʻonani--Juvenile fiction. 2. Wong-Kalu, Hinaleimoana--
Juvenile fiction. I. Song, Mika, illustrator II. Title.

PZ7.1.G35Ho 2019   j823'.92   C2018-906266-5
                                                C2018-906267-3

Published simultaneously in the United States of America by Tundra Books of Northern New York, an imprint of Penguin Random House Canada Young Readers, a Penguin Random House Company

Library of Congress Control Number: 2018962661

Edited by Samantha Swenson
Designed by John Martz
The artwork in this book was rendered in watercolor and ink.
The text was set in Plantin.
Hawaiian language consultant: Bryson Kainoa Embernate

This book was inspired by the film *A Place in the Middle*, produced by Dean Hamer and Joe Wilson, featuring story by Hinaleimoana Kwai Kong Wong-Kalu. Aplaceinthemiddle.org

Printed and bound in China

www.penguinrandomhouse.ca

1   2   3   4   5   23   22   21   20   19

Penguin
Random House
tundra | TUNDRA BOOKS

AUTHOR'S NOTE

The main character in the book you are about to read is based on a real person: Hoʻonani Kamai. Hoʻonani was born and raised in Kalihi Valley, a neighborhood in Honolulu, Hawaiʻi. Hoʻonani loves music and, just like her character in the story, plays a mean ukulele!

Hoʻonani's coach in the story, Kumu Hina, is also a real person: Hinaleimoana Kwai Kong Wong-Kalu. Kumu Hina (kumu means teacher!) is a Kānaka Maoli teacher, a Hawaiian cultural practitioner, a community leader, an activist and the first transgender candidate to run for statewide political office in the United States.

Both Hoʻonani and Kumu Hina were involved in the documentary *A Place in the Middle*, which this book is based on. You can watch it here: aplaceinthemiddle.org.

Dean Hamer and Joe Wilson, the producers of the documentary, were inspired by Kumu Hina and her "great effort to create a school environment where all kids are welcome and feel like they belong . . . Hina has created a special 'place in the middle' for students who might be marginalized and mistreated elsewhere."

We hope that you are inspired by Kumu Hina and Hoʻonani too!

In ancient Hawaiian culture, every person had a role in society. Māhū, people who embraced both feminine and masculine traits, were valued as healers and as caretakers and teachers of ancient traditions.

In *Hoʻonani: Hula Warrior*, we hope to show that, in the spirit of this Hawaiian tradition, we can make room for all people — kāne, wahine, māhū — and show every person the same unconditional acceptance and respect.

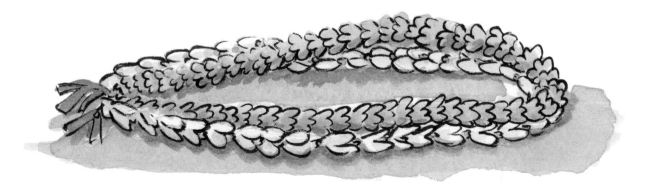

Hoʻonani Kamai did not see herself as a wahine, "girl."

Or think she was a kāne, "boy."

She preferred just Hoʻonani.

"She is who she is!" her mother said.

"She does what she wants!" her father said.

But her sister, Kana, wished Ho'onani did not sing songs so loud or play ukulele faster and better than every kāne at school.

One morning, Hoʻonani's teacher, Kumu Hina, made an announcement. This year they would bring a Hawaiian custom back to the community.

"Our high-school kāne will perform a traditional hula chant," she said.

Closing her eyes, Hoʻonani could almost smell smoke from the driftwood fire,

hear feet stomp-stomp-stomping,

see fingers tap-tap-tapping

and palms pitter-pat-patting.

She sighed.

If only she were kāne AND old enough for high school . . .

Then Hoʻonani heard,

"Auditions."

Ho'onani could not wait to tell her family!

"There'll be three tests," she said. "And Kumu Hina thinks I should try out."

Her father, mother and brothers were not surprised.

Kana rolled her eyes. "Really?"

Ho'onani wanted to say she could not believe it either.

But before she could speak, her sister changed the subject.

The next day, Ho'onani jogged to the gym.

She peered inside.

Strolling down the line, Kumu Hina inspected each kāne's stance.

On her command, their arms rose, bending at the elbows.

When Kumu Hina pushed down hard to measure warrior strength, Ho'onani's breath quickened.

She should be with them!

Her mind made up, she strode inside.

One by one,
their faces changed.

A wahine!

A wahine?

Not a wahine?!

Last in line, Hoʻonani lifted her arms.

As Kumu Hina pushed down, she held her place.

Strong,

sure,

and steady.

Ho'onani could not stop grinning when she told her family she passed.

Kana frowned. "How embarrassing!"

Her words made Ho'onani's chin tremble.

She wanted to ask Kana if they could ride bikes again,
like they used to.

But before she could speak, her sister had turned away.

Memorizing the sway and song of story took
patience and practice.

Ho'onani did not stop until Hawai'i's history
was part of her, in dreams by night, and
thoughts by day.

Hands dragging across her face, arms reaching
for the sky.

As Ho'onani called the sun, the moon, the stars,
she held her place.

Strong,

sure,

and steady.

Finally, it was time to choose a leader.

Hoʻonani's stomach twisted
in nervous knots.

One kāne, another,
and then another,
stepped forward.

Hoʻonani studied them.

Who was nervous,
or worried?

Who stood tall,
who slouched?

Who stayed focused,
and who squirmed?

Then, her turn!

Faces swam in front of Hoʻonani as she called for attention, "Ohhh aye ohhh . . ."

She paused.

Would they follow her?

No time to think. Words pushed against her lips and the chant tumbled out,

"'Ai ka mūmū kēkē,"

sweeping her warriors into a tidal wave of voices, until Hoʻonani called the end.

"Hai alla, hai alla, eh-oi-ay!"

Silence hung in the air.

When Hoʻonani saw complete awe and true acceptance, she held her place.

Strong,

sure,

and steady.

She was their leader.

Later, Kumu Hina beckoned her over.

Her teacher spoke with respect and honesty.

She said some might not appreciate a wahine leading their sons up on stage.

They might create a fuss.

Ho'onani knew she could not quit now. She had earned this position.

She thought of her sister and looked up at Kumu Hina.

"If someone wants to leave," she said, "that is their problem."

That evening, Ho'onani couldn't wait to tell her family she had been chosen as leader of the kāne hula troupe. Her parents and brothers were proud. But Kana wasn't.

"Why do you always have to reject wahine things?" Kana said.

"Just because I feel more kāne doesn't mean I'm not wahine! I'm in the middle! Why can't you let me be me?"

Before Kana could speak, Hoʻonani left the table.

At last, the day of the show arrived.

People lined up, tickets in hand.

Chatter overflowed the hall.

Lights dimmed.

Ho'onani wanted to feel strong, sure and steady. But she was nervous.

What if she wasn't kāne enough?

If people protested, what would she do?

From behind the curtain, a voice boomed.

"... The next day, the island shook violently.
Tūtū Pele erupted from the depths."

"Oli!" Ho'onani shouted back on cue.
Ready or not, it was time.

And to the beat of drums,

the thud of heels,

the clack of sticks,

she toe-heel stomped across the stage.

Ho'onani faced the crowd.

Her skin prickled.

She felt their curiosity stir the darkness, but she held her place.

Strong,

sure,

and steady.

ka mūmū kēkē

Her voice thundered.

The crowd gasped with
appreciation and roared
with approval.

One person stood.

Hoʻonani caught her breath . . . Kana?!

Hoʻonani had found her place.

Not as a wahine,

not as a kāne,

but as a

hula warrior.